JUN 2016

For Nola Godwin—a wise and punny lady!
—T. G.

For Lillian, the happiest guppy I know
—N. N.

Flip & Fin: Super Sharks to the Rescue!
Copyright © 2016 by HarperCollins Publishers
All rights reserved. Manufactured in China. For information address HarperCollins Children's Books,
a division of HarperCollins Publishers, 195 Broadway, New York, NY 10007.
www.harpercollinschildrens.com

Watercolors were used to prepare the full-color art.
The text type is 30-point Beton T Bold.

Library of Congress Cataloging-in-Publication Data

Gill, Timothy, (date) author.
Flip & Fin : super sharks to the rescue! / by Timothy Gill ; illustrated by Neil Numberman.
pages cm.—(Flip & Fin)
"Greenwillow Books."
Summary: When sand shark twins Flip and Fin try to rescue people and save the day
like the heroes of their favorite cartoon, there is a misunderstanding.
ISBN 978-0-06-224301-0 (trade ed.)
[1. Sand tiger shark—Fiction. 2. Sharks—Fiction. 3. Superheroes—Fiction. 4. Twins—Fiction.
5. Brothers—Fiction.]  I. Numberman, Neil, illustrator.
II. Title. III. Title: Flip and Fin, super sharks to the rescue! IV. Title: Super sharks to the rescue!
PZ7.G3995Flc 2016  [E]—dc23  2014041234

16  17  18  19  20  SCP  10  9  8  7  6  5  4  3  2  1
First Edition
Greenwillow Books

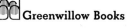

# Flip & Fin

## Super Sharks to the Rescue!

BY

**Timothy Gill**

ILLUSTRATED BY

**Neil Numberman**

Greenwillow Books

Here comes Flip.

Here comes Fin.

# Flip and Fin, the sand shark twins.

On Saturday morning, Flip and Fin watched their favorite cartoon.

Sammy Saw Shark and Harry Hammerhead zipped and flipped. They leaped high in the air. They caught bad guys. They saved the day.

**Faster than a sailfish! Tougher than a clamshell!**

"Do you think we could save the day?" asked Flip.

"Someone out there must need our help," said Fin.

"Let's go find him," said Flip.

SUPER SHARKS TO THE RESCUE!

Fin slipped through the waves. Flip zipped along beside him.

"Hey, Fin," said Flip. "What's a superhero's favorite part of a joke?"

"I don't know," said Fin.

"The punch line!" said Flip.

"Ha-ha, good one, Flipster," said Fin. "Now, no more jokes.
We've got a job to do."

Flip and Fin raced around the coral reef.

They spotted Swimmy and Molly.

"We are going on an adventure," said Flip. "A super shark adventure."

"We'll come, too," said Molly.

"Yes," said Swimmy. "We'll all be super sharks. Race you to the surface!"

At last they reached the surface.

Fin zipped through the water.

Fin zipped here. He zipped there.

"I am Sammy Saw Shark," said Fin.

Zip. Zip. Zip.

Fin's fin sliced through the waves.

Flip watched Fin zipping about.

"Too much zipping," he said. "Time for some flipping."

Flip flipped. He did a double flip. Then a triple.

"Fliptastic," said Swimmy.

"Fliptacular," said Molly.

"Far flippin' out!" said Fin. "Just like Harry Hammerhead!"

"Watch this," Flip said. "I'm going to do a super-duper quadruple flip."

Flip flipped.

But the flip flopped.

Flip landed on his noggin . . .

right on top of something bouncy!

"Hey, what's this?" asked Flip.

"This thing belongs to the human people," said Fin.

"All day long, the human people chase after it," said Fin.

"They must like it very much," said Flip. "They must be looking for it."

"We can take it to them," said Fin. "The human people will thank us."

We will be heroes.

Flip and Fin tossed the ball to Swimmy and Molly.

Back and forth. Up and down.

The four friends swam toward the shore.

"Greetings, human people!" yelled Fin.

"Look what we found," shouted Flip.

He balanced the ball on his nose. He tossed it in the air.

He caught it with his tail.

For as long as it took a horsefly to zap Fin's snout, there was silence. Then . . .

The humans swam and splashed and stumbled for the shore.

"Humans! Humans!" called Fin.

"Come back."

Flip swam as fast as he could
toward the nearest one.
"I'll save you!" he yelled.

"Stop, Fin!" said Molly. "Stop, Flip!
 I think the human people are afraid."

"Afraid?" said Flip.

"Afraid?" said Fin. "Why are they afraid?"

Flip looked at Fin. Fin looked at Flip.

"Oh! Now we see," said Flip and Fin.

"The human people are afraid of the stripey ball!"

"Don't worry, humans," said Flip.

"We are super sharks. We will save you."

Flip flipped the ball in the air.

Fin hit the ball with his tail.

Flip leaped up and

caught the ball in his mouth. . . .

Flip spit the ball out.

The ball wobbled through the air and landed far out to sea.

"The stripey ball can't hurt you now," said Fin.

"Our work here is done," said Flip.

Flip raised his fin. So did Fin.

Swimmy and Molly waved.

The four friends headed for home.

"Silly human people," said Flip.

"They were afraid of the stripey ball."

"But we saved them," said Fin. "We are heroes!"

"Let's race!"

**Sand sharks look very scary, but they aren't.**
Sand sharks have three rows of teeth that go every which way,
even sticking out when their mouths are closed. But they are
usually not aggressive and won't bother humans unless
the humans bother them.

**Sand sharks shed their teeth.**
Every two weeks or so, sand sharks shed all their teeth. Some can go through
as many as 30,000 teeth in their lifetimes. That's a lot of loose teeth!

**Sand sharks got their name because they like to be near the beach.**
Sand sharks like living in shoreline habitats. They can often be seen very close to the beach,
in warm waters all over the world, swimming along the ocean floor.

**Sand sharks can detect electrical signals emitted by muscle contractions of their prey.**
Sand sharks have special organs on the sides of their heads that detect electrical signals.
Because of this special sense, they can hunt for food even in murky water.

**Sand sharks swallow their food whole.**
Sand sharks eat mostly small fish, but they will also eat other sea animals,
such as crustaceans or even squid.

**A sand shark will grow to be bigger than you.**
Sand sharks grow to between six and ten feet long. They can weigh up to 350 pounds.
Scientists recently discovered that they can live up to forty years in the wild.